D1230617

MY FRIEND SUE

MY FRIEND SUE

by
P. CATHERINE COLES

VICTORY PRESS

EASTBOURNE

© Victory Press, 1976

ISBN 0 85476 244 2

Printed in Great Britain for
VICTORY PRESS (Evangelical Publishers Ltd.)
Lottbridge Drove, Eastbourne, E. Sussex BN23 6NT
by Richard Clay (The Chaucer Press), Ltd.,
Bungay, Suffolk

CONTENTS

CHAPTER ONE

THE START OF THE STORY

Sue Moorland wasn't always my best friend but she is now, and how we came to be friends is what this story is all about. I'm Janey Townsend, but I couldn't call this *The Story of Janey* without sounding stuck on myself. Anyway, like all good stories, this one has a happy-ever-after ending and that is nearly all due to Sue and me being friends.

In the old days when we lived in Millbury, Sue's father was our doctor. He used to say he had known all us children in the village since we were 'no-high', and he was about right. New people didn't often come to Millbury because there wasn't any work to do there and no one was building any new houses for them to live in. In those days I don't think Dr Moorland and his wife would have chosen me as a friend for their Sue, because I was not a very nice child.

Ours was not what I would call a very nice family. we were quite respectable—we didn't beat each other up or get into debt or anything like that—but we weren't a real family all together in the home. Daddy had been out of work for ages and then got a job in France so we didn't see him very often, and Mummy had to work, too, so we didn't see as much of her as most children see of their mothers. With Dad away and Mum out so much, Louise, my older sister, got very bossy and that always did something to me so that my prickles came out and I did and said stupid things just to show I didn't care—only really I did care. But this won't be a proper story if I don't go back to the beginning, and that means to the time when I was about ten.

At that time Louise was eleven and a half and Joe

was five. When we went off to school in the mornings
Mum gave Louise the key on a string round her neck
so that we could get in at four o'clock, as she didn't
get home till the bus came in at a quarter to five.
Every time Louise took that key from Mum she got
just that bit more bossy; she felt superior anyway
because she could remember the time before Dad lost
his job. He had worked in Rickston, five miles away,
and we had lived in a bigger house then, near Dr
Moorland. Mum had been home all day then and we
had had a car and a caravan. I only just remember
that time because I was only three when we moved
down to the other end of the village, into a poky little
house in a row of other poky little houses, and Daddy
was out of work for ages because the people he
worked for used all their money and couldn't make
any more, so they stopped being a firm and sent home
all the people who worked for them. Even though
Daddy wasn't working we had lots of fun then and I
didn't mind not being in the big house or having
the car, because we were happy as we were. I don't
suppose Mummy and Daddy were all that happy but
we didn't know that. Joe wasn't born then so he only
remembers Daddy being away nearly always and the
crazy fun we had when he came home for a holiday.

Apart from the times when Dad came home or we
visited our grandparents, life was not very exciting.
Things seemed to happen somewhere else to other
people—according to the TV anyway—but nothing
ever happened to us. And then one day things did
begin to happen. In one way it was my fault.

It started on a hot, stuffy Friday afternoon in school.
Friday afternoons always seemed longer and hotter
and stuffier than other afternoons. I kept looking at
the clock, feeling sure it must have stopped. Upstairs,
class three were having a singing lesson, and out in
the hall a P.E. teacher was taking class five and they
were jumping and thudding about like elephants.

Our window was open and in the road outside three women were having a good old gossip, loud enough to make you listen but not loud enough to let you hear what they were saying. In our room there were twenty-two of us humped over our desks trying to write a composition. You had to concentrate hard if you wanted to write a composition that would please Miss Johnson, and most of us did want to, because we liked Miss Johnson. But that afternoon we couldn't concentrate properly because of what had happened, and that's the bit that was my fault—I'll admit that now, but I wouldn't then. At the time I only shrugged my shoulders and thought Chrissie was daft to keep on sniffling over a biro she had lost and got back again, and Miss Johnson was mean to be sarcastic to me in front of all the class.

Chrissie had been given the biro for her birthday the previous week and when she went to get it to start her composition it wasn't in her school bag or her desk and she started sniffling, so, of course, Miss Johnson wanted to know what was the matter. The trouble was Miss Johnson made us all open our desks for inspection and Chrissie's biro was in my desk—well, I had put it there, but then I had found it on the floor so it would have got trodden on if I hadn't picked it up. The trouble is that it wasn't the first time I'd been found with other people's things in my desk or school-bag. I didn't ever mean to steal but I had a way of finding things that no one else seemed to notice, and then I picked them up. I'd never go and take anything out of someone's pocket or bag, but when I'd found something I'd look at it and like it and like the feel of it. I always meant to hand them in as lost property but someone found out before I did and then there was trouble. It was no use explaining to Miss Johnson. I think she was too nice herself to understand. That day when she took Chrissie's biro out of my desk she gave me a really nasty look—you know that grown-ups' look of 'what-would-your-mother-say'—and then she said that I had better remember that there were other kinds of schools for children who wouldn't stop taking other people's things, and if I wasn't careful I might find myself there one day.

I pretended I didn't care and started my writing but I did care really, and I didn't like the way Sue, who was next to me, looked at me and moved her school bag from between us on the floor to the other side of her chair. I could just see her going home and telling her mother all about that dreadful Janey Townsend and what Miss Johnson had said. Somehow I didn't like the idea of that. I'd been taken to Dr Moorland once when I fell through a window and cut my arm, and he had been marvellous. After he had stitched me up Mrs Moorland gave us cups of lovely hot, sweet tea and took us into her kitchen to drink it. It was a super kitchen—the kind I want when I'm married and have my own home—all blue and white matching things and tiles and shiny sinks and gadgets. I'd never grumble about washing up or peeling the potatoes in a kitchen like that.

At last the school bell rang and we were all rushing out to get our coats. Once we were round the corner Louise and Joe and I slowed down. We were never in a great hurry to get home, because with Mum not home until later old Mr and Mrs Brown across the road kept an eye on us for her and we didn't much like them. They were quite nice really but Louise didn't like them because she thought she could look after us by herself. I didn't like them because they told tales on us to Mum and because they thought I should run errands for them whenever they wanted me to.

"Come on, it's Friday!" Louise called to me as I dawdled behind, and as Joe started running on I had to hurry, too. If we could all hurry together over the last bit of the road we could sometimes slip in before the Browns noticed, and we'd glow with triumph if we made it, especially if it had been difficult and we'd had to dodge back a bit before we could get in unseen.

We liked Friday evenings. Mum would bring home hot fish and chips ready for our tea, so Louise and I only had to lay the table and fill the kettle. Other days we had to peel potatoes, too. Mum didn't go to work on Saturdays or Sundays, so Friday evenings were different; Mum wasn't rushing round getting things done all the time. We took longer over tea and then, when we'd all washed up together, she'd wash our hair and we'd sit round the table and play games or just chatter while she dried our heads.

We hurried home on that particular Friday but I wasn't all that happy. I had seen Chrissie's big sister talking to Louise in the cloakroom, and Chrissie was with them so I could guess what that meant: Louise would be told all about the biro affair, and she was bound to tell Mum and then I'd be in more trouble.

CHAPTER TWO

TROUBLE ALL ROUND

Mum was hardly inside the house that Friday before there was a bang on the front door. She had just laid down the brown paper packet of fish and chips, and was unbuttoning her coat. We all groaned loudly. Even Mum didn't really want a visitor at teatime on a Friday. She went out to the door and we all listened anxiously.

"Oh, you are home! I thought I saw you."

It was the unwelcome voice of Mrs Brown.

"Now what?" I demanded rudely, eyeing the parcel on the kitchen dresser.

Louise took over as usual.

"Hush, Janey! She'll hear you. Here, get out the plates and we'll put Mum's in the oven. She won't mind if we start, and the kettle's just going to boil."

Very carefully, with absolute fairness Louise divided out the food, smacking my knuckles sharply when I tried to direct a few extra chips on to my plate.

"Fair's fair, greedy!" she said in her grown-up sort of voice.

I grinned. It was never any use battling with Louise and I had to admit that although she often served out meals for us she never took more than a fair share for herself. I think I probably would have kept more for myself if I had been sharing out things like chips or ice-cream or cake.

We were busy eating when Mum came back. We could see at once that she was upset about something. Louise sprang up and fetched her plate from the oven. Mum only muttered her thanks and poured herself out a cup of tea. She gulped some of it down quickly, tried to take a bit of fish and then pushed her plate to one side.

"What's wrong, Mum?"

Joe had slipped out of his place and gone to stand close to her. He hated seeing anyone unhappy. Mum took another drink of tea and then blew her nose. She put an arm round Joe and drew him towards her.

"It's Gran. She's been taken ill. Grandpa phoned to Mrs Brown, and I don't know what I ought to do."

Gran was Mum's mother. Daddy's parents were always called 'Dad's mum' and 'Dad's dad'. They lived in New Zealand and did not seem like real people to us children. But Gran and Granda Murray were very real to us—as real as our own mum and dad. They lived only about fifty miles away and quite often we stayed with them, sometimes for the weekend but always during school holidays and especially at Christmas.

Louise looked troubled.

"What can we do to help, Mum?" she asked, and I wanted to say the same thing, but Louise always got in first.

"I'm not sure yet. Aunty Jill thinks I ought to go over there tomorrow, but we can't all go—that would be too much for them with Gran ill. Mrs Brown says she could keep Louise and Joe."

"I'll come, Mum. Janey and Joe can stay. I'm the eldest."

"I'll come; the girls can stay."

Louise and Joe both spoke together. I said nothing because I knew Mum would arrange it the way she wanted it anyway.

"Sorry, my dears, I know you'd like to come, but I also know that you won't give Mrs Brown any trouble."

"And I suppose I will!" I flashed out without stopping to think how Mum must be feeling.

"You might, Janey. You do have a way of getting

into trouble, don't you?" Mum looked at me then and I looked at my plate.

"She's been in trouble already today," Joe chipped in. Much as he hated people to be unhappy he hadn't realised yet that he could help them sometimes just by keeping his mouth shut. Louise signed to him to be quiet, but it was too late.

"What trouble?" Mum looked straight at me.

I shrugged my shoulders.

"Well?"

Joe, silenced by Louise, said nothing. I said nothing. Mum looked at Louise.

"Chrissie Black lost her new biro and Miss Johnson found it in our Janey's desk—but I don't like telling tales, Mum."

"I know, Louise my dear, and if Janey would own up you wouldn't have to. It settles tomorrow. I can't leave you with anyone, Janey, when you take things that don't belong to you. I've spoken to you before and so has Daddy. You know that quite well and you know that nice people don't take what does not belong to them. Now, clear the table, like good children, and settle down quietly to something until I get back. I must go over and phone Aunty Jill."

Mum stood up and drank the last dregs of her tea. I don't know what possessed me but I felt all horrid and black and nasty inside.

"Mum, can I have your chips?"

I don't know what made me say it or how I could. Louise and Joe pounced on me angrily.

"You greedy little horror! How can you, and when Mum's so worried? I'm putting her plate back into the oven for when she comes back."

Louise reached for the plate and Joe grabbed me as I put out my hand. There was a crash—and then a horrible silence. We three children stood looking at a broken plate, a broken cup and saucer, tea trickling over the tablecloth and staining it, and a mass of

broken china and cold, greasy fish and chips in a heap
on the carpet.

Mum strode back into the room and exploded at us.
"Children! How can you?"

Louise sprang into action and dived into the cupboard for a dustpan and brush and some old news-
papers. Mum was really upset now and we couldn't
blame her. She grabbed the things from Louise and
swept away the mess, clattering it into the dustbin
and banging the back door.

"Now!" she said when she came in again. "Upstairs
this minute and lie down on your beds, all of you, and
no talking till I get back. Now—I mean it; understand?"

We were three very subdued children slinking away
upstairs. When Mum had watched us go she went over
to Mrs Brown to phone Aunty Jill. Lying on my bed
I felt miserable. It was a good thing Mum had told
us not to talk, because Louise would have had plenty
to say to me. I heard her slip into Joe's room though
I kept my eyes shut. I could guess she was going to
cuddle him up and comfort him a bit, and I was glad.
Neither she nor Joe would talk when Mum had said
not to, but it had been my fault, and I didn't want
Joe to be miserable.

It was more than an hour later when Mum called
to us to come down. Three mugs of cocoa stood on
the table and a plate of bread and butter.

"Mum, I'm sorry," Louise began.

"It's all right, dear; it was an accident and I was
sharp because I was worried about Gran and about
you, Janey. Now, I've a lot to do and I want you to go
to bed as soon as you've had your cocoa. You can take a
book and read until I come up to tuck you in. We'll
need to be up early tomorrow. Here's your pocket-
money. Louise, please take care of Joe and help Mrs
Brown all you can. Joe, mind and don't give any
trouble, will you, pet? Here's your money, Janey,

though I've a good mind not to let you have it this
week. You won't get it if there's a next time, so remember that. Now, upstairs as soon as you are
finished."

We didn't take long over our cocoa, and Louise and
Joe both kissed Mum when we got up and had rinsed
out our mugs at the sink. I ought to have done the
same and been nice to her and told her how sorry I
was. But I've already told you I wasn't a nice child,
and it's true. I snatched up my pocket-money and
marched out of the room without a word, and then
sulked upstairs when Louise tried to be the reprov-
ing big sister to me.

CHAPTER THREE

GRAN AND GRANDA

Louise was still feeling subdued when we got up next morning. She and Joe waved goodbye to us and I knew that she would take as long as she could making the beds and washing the dishes. She would like to spin the work out to last all morning, but Joe would be impatient to go because Mr Brown always made a fuss of him. I knew Louise still felt that it was unfair that I was the one to get taken to Gran and Granda, just because I couldn't be trusted to be good while Mum had to be away.

My day was very different. We none of us knew anything about serious illness but I knew that Mum was worried as we travelled together so I sat quiet and didn't ask any questions. For one thing, I did not want to start her off about my behaviour the previous day. Perhaps by Monday the fuss would have blown over at school, especially if I could silence Louise and Joe. I felt in my pocket and dug out my pocket-money. Perhaps I could slip into a shop and buy some sweets to take home to them to help make up for to-day— and that might also keep them quiet about that other affair.

When we arrived at the house I was surprised, because usually we got such a welcome from Gran and Granda and Aunty Jill. This time the house was very quiet. Granda opened the door, patted me on the head and spoke to Mum. Mum pushed me into the kitchen and shut the door. Lots of my favourite books were on the table and a mug of milk and some biscuits, so I supposed I was meant to sit there and read. It was all right for a bit, but I heard people moving

about upstairs and car doors banging and voices and
I began to feel forgotten and lonely. Just when I felt
I could not bear the strange silence any longer the
door opened and there was Aunty Jill. I flung myself
at her.

"Oh Aunty Jill!" I cried. "What is going on?"

"You poor old Scrap! Did you think we'd forgotten
all about you?" Aunty Jill and the grandparents were
the only people who still used that name for me.
"Come and help me get the lunch ready, will you?"

I ran about the kitchen eagerly fetching basins and
tins and spoons and saucepans, peeling potatoes and
watching the milk-pan boil. As we worked together I
asked all the questions that had been bottled up inside me all morning.

"How is Gran? Is she very ill? What is the matter
with her?"

Aunty Jill went on with the cooking, answering
me as she worked.

"Yes, Janey dear, I'm afraid Gran is very ill at
present."

"But I can see her?" I pleaded. "Does she know
I've come?"

"You can't see her for a while yet, I'm afraid."

"Why not?" I said, and I don't think I said it very
nicely. I wanted to see Gran.

"For one thing she is too ill, for another only
Granda will see her for the next few days, I expect,
and for another she has been taken away to hospital."

"Oh! When?" I asked.

"Just a little while ago. Granda and your mummy
have gone with her in the ambulance, but they will
be back soon and I want to have lunch ready for
them."

I had almost stopped listening to Aunty Jill. I was
remembering all the excitement in our street when
little Kenny Briggs had been taken away by ambulance. And now my very own Gran had been taken,

and I had been shut away in the kitchen and hadn't seen any of it. It would have been a marvellous story to tell at school on Monday: how Gran had looked, all white and still lying on the stretcher, and how Mum and Granda had gone in beside her crying, just like Mrs Briggs. Though I knew neither Mum nor Granda would be crying out in the street, but it made the story sound much more interesting. I stood staring out of the window, not seeing the flowers and trees, but seeing myself at school and the others goggle-eyed listening to me. Perhaps I could still tell it, if Mum didn't go and tell Louise and Joe about me being kept out of the way all morning.

Aunty Jill mistook my silence for sadness.

"Don't fret, Scrap," she said gently.

I turned round slowly. I was remembering that Kenny Briggs' going to hospital was not the biggest excitement. Kenny Briggs had not got better and there had been a huge funeral with masses of flowers. I could still see myself telling the children at school about Gran. I looked Aunty Jill straight in the face and asked the most important question.

"Will Gran die?"

At that moment Mum came in and heard me.

"Janey!" she said in her most shocked tone of voice.

I jumped guiltily but Aunty Jill went on calmly straining the potatoes and beating in a generous dab of butter.

"We don't know, Scrap," she said in her usual unruffled voice. "We hope not, because we want her with us for as long as possible. We do have to remember that God takes care of all these things and He only does what is best for us." She turned to Mum and said, "It's all right, Ellen; the children are bound to ask questions."

Mum still looked a bit cross.

"Well, Janey, don't go asking them in front of Granda, that's all."

I took the hint, and as I could hear Granda coming downstairs I went back quietly to helping Aunty Jill and kept my mouth shut.

After lunch the grown-ups wanted to sit on and talk. Granda put his hand into his pocket and took out some shiny coins and gave them to me, and Mum told me I could go down to the shop at the corner and buy something, and I could have a few swings in the park on the way back so long as I was home in half an hour. I slipped away quickly. This was better than I had dared hope for. At the station it had been impossible to suggest buying sweets. Mum had taken my hand and we had rushed past everything in her haste to get to Gran. Now I had time given to me and money to spend.

I flattened my nose on the window, trying to make up my mind what to buy. In spite of being bad in lots of ways I was fond of Louise and Joe and I did really like sharing anything good that came my way. When I did do wrong it was nearly always because I didn't think before I did something or said something —that was my trouble. And then when I'd been bad I felt sorry but I could never come to the point of saying so. Louise could, and things blew over quickly for her, but I would go on and on adding one trouble to another.

I studied the window carefully and then went inside. I bought a bright tube of Smarties for Joe, a Mars bar for Louise, mints for Gran and Granda, and jelly babies for Aunty Jill and Mummy. That left four pence. What should I get? There were so many things to choose from and I liked them all. I liked chewy sweets and sticky sweets and nutty sweets. I liked the kind you can suck and they last for a long time. I liked licorice and toffee and gum. Then, quickly before I could change my mind, I bought a little packet of the kind that Chrissie likes. Triumphantly I stuffed them into my pockets and left the shop feeling very warm and comfortable because I had been generous and spent all my money on other people.

The house was very quiet again when I went back. I pushed open the kitchen door and walked in. I knew I wasn't late, because I had watched the church clock very carefully and I had run all the way home just to be sure. Tea was laid in the kitchen and Mum's coat and bag were on the chair just inside the door. The kettle was beginning to sing and I wasn't surprised to hear Aunty Jill come running downstairs calling that tea was ready and Janey was back.

Carefully I laid out the sweets for Gran and Granda, Aunty Jill and Mum, and glowed with happiness at the hugs and kisses I got in return. Then Mum told me the news. She was going home to Louise and Joe but I was to stay with Granda and Aunty Jill. It was too exciting to believe just at first. I loved Mum and Louise and Joe and our home, but there was no one quite like Granda and Aunty Jill; and to be allowed to stay with them by myself, and in term-time, too, was beyond all my day-dreams. It was just a little bit disappointing to remember that I would not be able to tell the others at school about Gran going in the ambulance, but then I remembered something else even better: if I wasn't going home I didn't need to give sweets to Louise and Joe and Chrissie. As I said —even when I was just a bit good, it didn't last long.

Half an hour later I stood between Aunty Jill and Granda and waved goodbye to Mum. I couldn't help being pleased about the way things had turned out for me. As we went indoors I slipped one hand into Aunty Jill's and one into Granda's. Mum had told me to be good and not give any trouble, and I was determined to try very hard this time.

Mum did not tell me that Grandpa had suggested it when he heard what I had been up to at school, nor that Aunty Jill had thought I might take Granda's thoughts off his own trouble if they had me with them. I only found those things out much later when I was older.

CHAPTER FOUR

CRABTREES

I have always loved every corner of Crabtrees, so I must tell you more about it. It was given its name long ago because it was built with orchards all round it and there were more crabapple trees than any other kind. Gran told us that in those days people always served crabapple jelly with roast pork. The house used to belong to Granda's own grandparents so it really is very old. Over the years it has had bits added to it, and the kitchen has been modernised so that it looks more or less like Mrs Moorland's kitchen. It now has electricity like all the other houses, but when Granda was a boy they used oil lamps and log fires, and his mother did the cooking on a big black range that had three ovens and a water boiler. Gran and Granda kept some of the old cooking pots, and in the kitchen Aunty Jill still uses a big black iron kettle and a lovely shiny copper preserving-pan, and on the top shelves there are iron saucepans and flat irons, and she still keeps things like flour and sugar in the old glazed pottery crocks—stone jars with lids. They are much nicer to use than some of the modern tins and packets—at least I think so.

The orchards have all been built on now so that Crabtrees is just one house in a road of houses, but it is a very pretty road with grass between the kerb and the pavement, and trees planted that are full of pink flowers all the spring. The other houses are modern-looking but Granda's is really old and quite different, and his garden has old trees and shrubs while the newer ones have little thin trees and small shrubs. At the back Granda has a larger garden and there is still the old part through a little gate which is a perfect place to play in. There are very old, twisty trees to climb and the swing Aunty Jill and Mummy and the uncles had when they were children, and there are all the little marked-out places where family pets have been buried. Granda's dog, Rusty—a lovely golden labrador with kind eyes—liked to lie out there in the sun, and Paula, the black and white cat, was never far away from him. They were great friends, and when Granda took Rusty for a long walk Paula would go too, as far as the end of the next garden, and then she would sit there and wait for them to come back.

The house itself is like a story-book house with odd little windows at half-landings, and back stairs and odd-shaped rooms. Right at the top of the house there are large attics, and the stairs that lead up to them are hidden behind a door which looks just like the cupboard doors. All sorts of treasures are stored up there and we thought it the very nicest place to play in on a wet day. Our uncles, Uncle John, Uncle Peter and Uncle Tom, all carved their initials in the old beams, and Louise and Joe and I have tried to do ours too. There are boxes of old toys and old dolls up there, old-fashioned albums of picture postcards, games and books, Christmas decorations, and boxes of flags and bunting that were used on special royal or national occasions.

The front windows upstairs look across over the roofs of other houses so that you can see the sparkle of the river in the wide estuary, and the back windows look out on to fields with sheep and cows, farmers ploughing or cutting hay, or trimming their hedges.

At the side of the garden there is a lane and a gate leads into it from the garden. In the wall beside the gate is a heavy iron ring and Granda told me that long ago before there were any cars the men who came to visit tied their horses' reins to the ring so that they would not run away. In the long grass beside it there is a worn old stone, and these men used to stand on it to mount their horses when they were ready to ride away again. I've stood on that stone with Granda holding me because it is slippy and not easy to balance on. I'd love to have swung on to the back of a horse and galloped gaily away.

Well, Crabtrees was now my home, and as I lay on a camp bed Aunty Jill put up for me beside her own I couldn't stop thinking how wonderful it was to be there. Crabtrees, up until then, had meant holidays and having to say goodbye and putting everything away until that far-off 'next time'. Now I was there, and I was part of it, and it was for every day.

On Monday morning Aunty Jill took me to Maybank Road Primary School—not very far away. She took me to the headmistress, and then left me to get on as best I could. I looked round with interest and I liked it. This school was new and exciting. The rooms were big and sunny and had large windows and bright-coloured walls. Miss Andrews took me along to class six and introduced me to Miss Watson the teacher. When Miss Andrews had gone Miss Watson found me a desk and gave me a new jotter and told Mary Martin to share her text book with me. Mary gave me a friendly grin and pushed her desk nearer to mine.

One happy week flew by, and then another. Soon I was really enjoying school for the first time. At Crabtrees I was even happier. I worked with Aunty Jill in the house and I never thought of grumbling about things like making my bed or helping wash up. I sat on Granda's knee and heard the latest news of Gran and sent her letters and drawings whenever Granda or Aunty Jill went to see her. And I was saving some of my pocket-money each week to buy her a real present when I was allowed to go and see her myself.

And then one night I woke to hear noises in the

house. I switched on the torch I kept by my pillow and saw that Aunty Jill's bed hadn't been slept in. I looked at my watch and it said ten past three. That was odd. I lay and listened for a while and then got up and quietly opened the door. There was a light in Granda's room and I could hear Aunty Jill's voice. I padded barefoot across the landing.

"Aunty Jill!" I called softly.

The voice stopped suddenly and Aunty Jill came out to me, her finger on her lips. She was still fully dressed and shepherded me silently back to our own room.

"What is it?" I asked in a whisper.

"Hop back into bed, Scrap, there's a good girl." She bent down and tucked me in. "Look, darling, the hospital has phoned to say that Gran is very ill again and Granda can go and sit beside her. I've got the car at the door and I'm just going to run him in and I'll come straight back. I won't be gone more than ten minutes. Now, I want you to stay where you are in bed —you can have the light on and Rusty will be here to keep you company—and as soon as I get back we'll have a cup of tea if you are still awake."

I snuggled down and promised to do what Aunty Jill said. I knew I could get the tea ready for her to come back to, but that would worry her and Mum had told me not to be a worry, and I was really trying to be good.

"Give Granda a kiss from me," I said as Aunty Jill hurried away.

"I will, Scrap," she called back, and they were gone.

The house was suddenly horribly quiet and ten minutes seemed a very long time. When Mum used to say 'ten minutes more and then up to bed' it seemed no time at all, but ten minutes when you are waiting and listening is more like half an hour. I was just beginning to feel so miserable that I was afraid I was going to start crying, when I heard the car come back and the sound of Aunty's Jill's key in the door. Then I heard her fill the kettle and the next minute she was calling to me from the foot of the stairs.

"Still awake, Janey?"

"Yes."

"Put on your dressing-gown and slippers and come down to the kitchen. It's warm and cosy down here."

I sprang out of bed and with Rusty at my heels we were soon sitting at the kitchen table. I knew Aunty Jill was unhappy and I tried to comfort her, but all the same there was something magic about drinking tea and munching bread and butter while all the neighbours' houses were in darkness and everyone else was in bed and asleep.

Next morning I found it hard to remember what had happened in the night, I was so sleepy; but when I got up and went downstairs I knew. Aunty Jill looked very tired and sad and there was no place laid for Granda at the breakfast table so I knew he must still be at the hospital. Aunty Jill gave me a note for Miss Watson and some money and asked me to have dinner at school that day. Staying at school for dinner could be quite fun but I didn't want to be away from Crabtrees and Granda all that day. I remembered just in time not to make a fuss and took the note and money and said nothing, kissing Aunty Jill and giving her an extra big hug before I set off.

I never dawdled on the way home now. The days at school were full of so much I wanted to tell at home and Aunty Jill and Granda were always there to welcome me and listen. Tea was usually ready and the evenings were every bit as good as the busy days. This afternoon I sped off the minute the bell rang. I wanted to get home quicker than ever to hear how Gran was, but when I ran up the back steps and let myself in by the kitchen door as usual I found Louise and Joe waiting for me. I noticed in a flash that tea was laid on the kitchen table just for three and it looked as if Louise had laid it.

For a moment I was shaken. Where was Aunty Jill? Where was Granda? *My* Aunty Jill and *my* Granda. And what was happening to Gran— *my* Gran? And why were Louise and Joe here? And why did they know more about everything? I felt hurt. I wasn't going to ask them anything. This was my home, anyway, now. I moved towards the door and Louise stopped me.

"You can't go, Janey. Mum and Aunty Jill said you were to stay here."

Unwillingly I had to hear it all from Louise and Joe because they wanted to tell me. Gran had died that morning, and Aunty Jill had sent for Mum and she had gone to the school and collected Louise and Joe and come straight over. Uncle Tom and Uncle John had arrived since, and Uncle Peter was due any minute. Louise made the tea and in sulky silence I sat down and ate some. It wasn't fair: I had been nearest to all this and yet I was the last to know what was happening.

Soon Mum came in and she had her coat on and was carrying Joe's and Louise's anoraks. It was so nice to see each other again, and of course I ran to give Mum a big kiss.

"Now!" she said, trying to sound a bit brighter than she looked, "Uncle John is going to run us all right home in his lovely big fast car; isn't that grand? Janey, you can go up to your room and get your things and say goodbye to Aunty Jill. Now mind," she added as she looked at me, "don't go making a fuss or upsetting her. And hurry, because Uncle John is driving straight back tonight."

I stood and stared.

"Me? Am I to come with the others?"

"Of course, dear. The uncles are all staying and that is more than enough for Aunty Jill."

"But I can help Aunty Jill; I know how she does things."

"Janey!"

Mum spoke sharply and I knew it was no use asking.

I went out of the room and upstairs. Aunty Jill was waiting for me on the landing and she just hugged me very tightly and whispered to me as we went into our room together.

"Come, Scrap. I wanted to have just a moment with you," she said gently. "I'm sorry it had to be this way; I wanted to tell you about Gran myself. You've been so good; will you go on now, doing all you can to help us even though we have to ask you to do it in a way you don't like so much? It still does help Granda and me very much; you know that, don't you?"

I nodded, but I couldn't speak.

Mum called me to hurry up, and we bundled my things together, and I hugged Aunty Jill again and went downstairs to the hall where the others were impatiently waiting for me.

CHAPTER FIVE

THE SCHOOL HOLIDAY

The one thing I dreaded never happened. All the way home I was thinking about having to go back to my old school and Miss Johnson and Chrissie. I had forgotten the term was nearly over, and there was only one more day of school so Mum let me stay home. She was staying at home, too, and we soon found out why. That evening Daddy arrived. Mum had sent him a telegram about Gran, and he had got his holiday dates changed, and he could be with us while Mum went back next day to be at Gran's funeral and help Aunty Jill.

Of course we were all sad about Gran, but a friend of Dad's lent him a car so we had an even better time than usual with him at home. It was a holiday to remember, especially once Mum was home too and we went for picnics and long days out in all sorts of interesting places. Then, just as suddenly, it came to an end. Louise and I began to notice those little signs that meant Dad was going away again. He started to put things into his big canvas hold-all, and Mum was in one of her moods so that she would let the milk boil over without noticing, and things like that. We hated those days. We wanted Dad with us all the time and I guess Mum wanted that even more than we did.

Daddy went off very early one morning when we had only a few days' school holiday left. We all got up to have breakfast with him and once he had gone the day stretched ahead, much longer than usual, because it was still only seven o'clock. Gloom was just beginning to settle on us when Mum startled us all.

"Now then, everyone; no loitering. We are off to

Crabtrees, and anyone not ready will just have to be left behind!"

Her words had a marvellous effect on us. Suddenly we were running about all over the place. Never were beds made so quickly, never were dishes washed and dried so fast. We dusted and packed up our few things and by ten o'clock we were ready with everything we could think of done. Louise had run along to the shops and cancelled the milk, and Mummy had spoken to the postman and been round the house securing all the windows.

"Fine!" she said as we all stood ready to get away.

Soon we were hurrying along the road eager to get to Crabtrees and Granda and Aunty Jill. Mum let us have a snack lunch at the station while we waited for the bus and then we were off.

Louise and Joe followed the route eagerly, picking out the familiar landmarks. I didn't say much. It was enough for me that we were going back to Granda and Aunty Jill. I wondered what it would be like without Gran, then I remembered Gran hadn't really been there all the time I was staying before. I wondered if Granda and Aunty Jill would be looking sad. Mum did quite often, and I didn't think that was only because Daddy had gone away again. I looked round at her sitting beside Joe in the seat behind and smiled, and she smiled back.

Soon we knew we were nearly there and began to gather up our coats and bags. Mum had to put a hand on Joe's shoulder or he would have been down the bus before it even stopped. When it did stop I managed to wriggle my way through and be out first—first into Aunty Jill's arms, first to get and give a welcome. I tried to get into the front seat of the car beside her but Louise was too sharp for me.

"Get out of there, Janey! You know Mum sits in front. Hurry up into the back."

Mum handed in our coats and things while Aunty

Jill put the bigger suitcase into the boot of her car, and we were soon driving away from the bus station in a burst of lovely spring sunshine. All along the roads the trees were coming into flower and the air smelt of that gorgeous mixture of salt from the sea, log smoke from the chimneys, and damp, mossy grass. When we got in, Granda was there to welcome us and we were soon sitting around the fire in his study, eating toasted buns and drinking tea.

For four long sunny days we enjoyed all the delights of Crabtrees. Granda took us out in the rowing-boat on the river, we climbed the downs and came home laden with fircones and dry wood to brighten up the fire after tea. We made toffee with Aunty Jill and sausage rolls with Mum. In the evenings we sat round the fire and sang songs while Aunty Jill played her guitar for us. And there were the old favourite books to read, and Ludo and Scrabble and Happy Families to play together.

And then it was the last day. The last morning of hot, scrunchy rolls for breakfast, the last row across the estuary, the last stop at the cafe for orange juice while Granda drank a cup of coffee. The last scramble over the downs. The last cosy tea round the fire with slabs of Aunty Jill's sticky brown gingerbread. The last sing-song and the last games before bed. I took as long as I could packing away the games box ready to put it back into the attic until that far-off next time. Then Granda called to me.

"Janey, ask your mother if you can come and sit with me for a few minutes before you go up to bed."

I flew upstairs like a shot.

"I can, Mum, can't I?" I begged when I had given Granda's message. I couldn't help noticing that Louise was looking a bit annoyed. Why should I get staying up longer? Perhaps I would tell her when I came up, and perhaps not; it would depend on what Granda wanted me for.

I gave Mum a big bear-hug and dashed back downstairs, taking the last three steps in one flying leap. Down in the study I perched on the arm of Granda's chair and leaned back against his shoulder.

"Were you happy here last term, Scrap?" he began.

"Happy!" How could I tell him how terribly, terribly happy I had been. "I was just the happiest ever, except about Gran."

He put his arm round me. He always seemed to understand what I meant.

"Your Aunty Jill and I were happy to have you. But you see, we are just two grown-ups and there are no other children in the home. Do you think you would go on being happy if you stayed a bit longer with us?"

"Happy, staying with you and Aunty Jill? Oh, Granda, of course I'd be happy. And I'd be very good—at least I would try very hard to be good. Do you think Mummy would mind? Do you think she would let me?"

I suddenly thought of Mummy and Louise and Joe and how that was really home and where I belonged. Maybe Mum would want it that way.

"Yes, Scrap, your mother will let you stay on if you want to stay."

"Just me?"

I knew it was a selfish question, but I had to ask it.

"Just you, Scrap, in term-time anyway. The others will all come in holiday time as usual. But Mummy would be lonely without any of you, wouldn't she? I've talked it over with your mother and your father, while he was at home, and Aunty Jill and I think it would be a good idea. You liked being at Maybank Road School, didn't you?"

I nodded vigorously. I was thinking about Judy and Mary and Miss Watson, and I was remembering Miss Johnson and Chrissie and the Browns and waiting for Mum to come home and Louise being bossy.

Granda took his arm away from my shoulders and, using both his kind old hands, he took hold of my face and turned it gently so that I could not try to look anywhere but straight into his eyes.

"I'm an old man, Scrap, but I see things, you know. You were not happy in your old school, were you?"

I went very red and tried to turn my face away but although his hands were gentle they were firm too and I had to look at him.

"Don't ever try to hide things from us, Janey. We only want to help you and you need never be afraid to tell me or your Aunty Jill or your Mummy when things are bothering you. How can we help if you won't let us, eh? Tell me, you have not felt the same way at school here have you?"

I shook my head.

"No; not ever; not even once, Granda. I don't feel bad and I don't want to be bad here. I feel good and then I want to be good."

"That's fine in a way, but you are old enough to know that we can all be good when things are going our way. That isn't much to be proud of. The really difficult thing is to be good when we feel like being bad and when things seem to be all against us. No one can do that alone and that is why we tell you about Jesus and His love, and how He came to die for us. Jesus can help us. Once we really love Him He can come and put His goodness inside us because He has promised never to leave us. I can't stand beside you at school to help you, but He can be with you, if you ask Him."

Granda must have noticed that I wasn't really listening. Perhaps he had noticed before that when he tried to talk to me seriously about being good and about loving Jesus I didn't listen properly. I heard the words he said but I didn't want to understand them. I wanted to be good by myself; I didn't want to admit that I couldn't be and I didn't want anyone to help me, not even Jesus. Granda didn't say any more about it. He kissed me goodnight and told me to run along up to bed and to be very kind to Mummy. He told me that she did not like having to go out to work to help Daddy make a home for us, instead of being at home all the time to make it an even nicer home.

I walked upstairs slowly. I was thinking. I knew Granda and Aunty Jill really did want me to stay but it had taken the edge off my joy just a bit to know that I was being allowed to stay because I behaved so badly at home and at my other school.

CHAPTER SIX

SUE MOORLAND

When I started this story I said that nothing exciting happened to us as a family. Once I settled down to being back at Crabtrees I suppose I could have said the same thing. I started to work harder at school because I wanted to; Miss Watson said I could if I tried, so I did try. I had Judy and Mary for my special friends, and although living with Granda and Aunty Jill was not exciting—not like the things that happen in stories or on TV—it was always busy and happy. There were so many things to do that were interesting and fun, so many new things to learn about, that I stopped looking for special adventures, and life seemed to me to be just about right.

There were thrilling holidays still when Daddy came home and all the family came to Crabtrees or I went to them for a few days. I didn't mind that now because I knew I would be coming back. Louise had moved on to the Gregg High School and she was more full of importance than ever. She wanted to take modern languages and already Daddy was talking about having her over in France for a holiday staying with his landlady's family. Joe was happy at anything and seemed to have been born contented.

Before long Judy and Mary and I were in our first year at Breakfield High School and we hardly noticed how the months and even years were passing. We had so much to do and we did nearly everything together. We camped and hiked and cycled; we swam and climbed and played games on Saturday mornings. We spent hours in each other's homes driving our respective families crazy with our choice of records, and sometimes we just got together and sat about and gossiped and giggled. Crabtrees was by far the nicest place to meet, and Aunty Jill let us make a proper den for ourselves in the attics. She only made one rule and that was 'no matches', which was reasonable when you think of all the dry wood in the roof, let alone all the treasures. Anyway, we didn't need matches, because she always let us make tea or coffee in the kitchen and take up what we wanted when we were up there.

One morning when everything was going well for me, I got a letter from Louise that really shook me. She wrote marvellous letters telling me all the odd bits of news from home, but this one was different.

"You'll never guess——" she wrote. "Sue Moorland's father has got an appointment at the hospital Gran was in. You'll remember Sue. She was in your class at Millbury. They must be moving quite soon but Sue left Gregg's today. I expect she will come to Breakfield so you'll be seeing her around. Isn't it a small world?"

I shivered. The last thing I wanted at Breakfield was for someone to turn up there from my bad old days—especially Sue. She knew too much about me. She had never been put off by my saying I had 'found' whatever it was that I had that belonged to someone else, and although nothing was ever said about it I was sure she suspected me when she lost a fifty-pence piece. As it happens she was right, and I had picked that up but I had got away with it that time. She knew better than to have money at school and her parents knew that, too, so they never made a fuss about it. I had meant to hand it over but nothing was ever said and not having done it right away made it harder to do later—so hard that I never did it. But I never fooled Sue, I was sure of that.

Now I was going to have to see Sue again just about every day. Even if she was not put into our class we were almost bound to meet quite often. I did not

have long to wait. Only two days later I saw her coming towards me down a long corridor. Fortunately I
knew my way around the school better than she did,
so I slipped out of sight behind some lockers and
waited until she had gone by. Time and time again
we were within speaking distance but I was always on
the look-out and managed to be talking to someone
else, or turning and going off in the other direction.

All the same, I wasn't happy about it. I was being
rude and I knew quite well that Sue had recognised
me from the start. And then she was moved into my
class.

School was only part of the trouble. The very first
Sunday after her arrival I walked into church with
Granda and Aunty Jill only to find the Moorlands
sitting about three rows in front of us and Sue was
wearing her school blazer over her dress.

"Who was the Breakfield girl, Janey? I don't remember seeing that family before and she looked
about your age."

Granda asked the question as we started lunch. I
had known he would, but even so I wasn't ready with
a good answer. I stuffed a piece of hot potato into
my mouth so that I could only mumble a reply.
Aunty Jill looked at me sharply and then she smiled
at me and changed the subject. She and I cleared up
after lunch without saying much to each other. We
were like that sometimes now, and it wasn't only over
Sue. I still loved Aunty Jill just as much as ever but
sometimes, coming home from school with Judy and
Mary, or after they'd been up in the attic with me
and we'd been making all sorts of plans for our lives,
Aunty Jill seemed to belong to a different world and
I couldn't expect her to understand all the things
that mattered so much to us. She was still the very
nicest person to be with—she and Granda—but they
were comfortable in a down-to-earth sort of way, not
like the marvellous dreams that Judy and Mary and

I had about all the places we would go to and the people we would meet and the fine jobs we would get. And of course the coming of Sue did make a difference. Sometimes I opened my mouth to tell Aunty Jill all about it, because I was so miserable inside, but I never did; I couldn't bear to think what she and Granda would feel about me if they really knew.

By the time Granda found out who the newcomers were, Sue and I were both avoiding each other deliberately. That was my fault. There were about seven hundred boys and girls at Breakfield and they came from all types of homes. The staff and prefects did do their best but at the moment there was a wave of petty thieving going on. We had all been warned not to leave things about in the cloakrooms or cycle-sheds, and appeals were made by class teachers for culprits to own up. This really bothered me. What would Sue be thinking? She must remember the old days, and suppose she told anyone about how I had been? With my own conscience bothering me I was ready to think she could do anything mean and spiteful to me.

Quite casually one day I dropped a hint or two to Judy and Mary. I told them we had had a spell of that sort of trouble at my old school. I also managed to mention that there was a girl from that school who had come quite recently. I persuaded myself that all I had said had been true, if Judy and Mary picked me up wrong that wasn't my fault. Or was it? My conscience gave me some more uncomfortable digs, especially when the girls took up my remarks and began to suggest things about Sue. I was wretched now. I had only meant to protect myself, but instead I had made trouble for Sue. My words had gone so much further than I meant them to and I could not now take them back.

It was just at this time that Granda met Dr Moorland at a hospital board meeting, and then within a

week they met again at a missionary meeting at the
church. Granda liked Dr Moorland and when they
met again, coming out of church the following Sunday morning, Aunty Jill invited the whole family to
tea that afternoon. I was frantic. After lunch I told
Aunty Jill that I had promised to meet Judy and
Mary and might be late home. Aunty Jill looked at
me and smiled.

"I don't think you have," she said.

"But I have!" I insisted.

"Then I think you've forgotten that they are both
away this weekend with their parents."

I could have kicked myself. I had been so busy
working out an escape for the afternoon that I had
forgotten that Aunty Jill, who took a bible class in
one corner of the big hall, could have seen that my
friends were missing from our class, or heard the
reason given when the roll was called. I flushed
angrily, and helped to lay the tea table in silence.
When we had finished I said I had a headache and
was going to my room. Aunty Jill let me go but a few
minutes later she tapped at my door—I had a small
room of my own now—and she came in with an
aspirin and a cup of tea.

"Drink this, Janey, and I should lie down for a bit.
We were all a bit late last night, weren't we?"

Left to myself I took the aspirin and drank the tea.
Aunty Jill was a pet but I could never, never tell her
what I was like on the inside. I sat and thought about
Sue and her parents. It was going to be horrible at
tea time. Perhaps if I lay down now I could pretend
to be asleep if Aunty Jill came looking for me and
she might leave me to sleep on. Then a worse thought
hit me. What would Sue tell them if I were not about?
She could ruin me completely in Granda and Aunty
Jill's eyes.

I lay down and watched the clock. I really had got
a headache now, and the sort of pain inside that no

aspirin could cure. At three o'clock I got up and went and washed my face. That made me feel a little bit better. Then I dressed again in my blue-grey pleated skirt and the blue jumper Aunty Jill had knitted for me. I fastened on the pendant Granda had given me for my last birthday. It was a single blue stone which matched my eyes, and it was set in silver and hung on a thin silver chain. My hair was shining and tidy and as I sat down to polish my nails I couldn't help knowing that I looked quite attractive—except for the frown that so often now made marks on my forehead. I got out my hand cream and manicure set. Aunty Jill never put any colour on her nails and I thought her hands were lovely, so I tried to keep mine like hers. Granda had given me Gran's little manicure set and I was very proud of it, partly because it had been Gran's and partly because I felt grown-up using it.

I was so busy that I forgot to watch the time and I did not hear the Moorlands' car. The sharp ring on the doorbell sent me flying downstairs determined not to leave our guests alone with Granda or Aunty Jill if I could help it.

It was the only unhappy meal I remember at Crab-trees. Sue and I were just polite to each other and no more. The adults had plenty to talk about but I knew they were all taking sideways looks at Sue and me and wondering what had got into us. When we rose from the table Sue offered to help clear away. Granda laid his hand on her shoulder.

"Not at all, my dear," he said. "Janey will help her aunt. You come and tell me all about yourself and how you like being here; I've hardly spoken to you yet."

So I had to watch Granda taking our guests through to his cosy study and the last I saw before the door closed was Granda giving Sue my special chair beside him. I was furious. I cleared the tea table tempestuously and, for the sake of her good china, Aunty Jill gave me other jobs to do while she washed and dried and put away her treasures. Usually I was pleased to help with her lovely things and liked handling them carefully and so far I had never broken anything. Today I could see she wasn't going to risk it.

The Moorlands did not stay very long after tea. Dr Moorland was going to make a call at the hospital and Mrs Moorland and Sue were going to the evening service. I had said I wasn't going and I couldn't change my mind when Aunty Jill said she was. Granda didn't often go out in the evenings now and I usually stayed in with him. I liked sitting quietly with a book while he played the old hymns that he loved on his piano. I did not bother much with the words but there was something rather romantic and moving about the log fire and the music and the old man who did not need music to play from, and I could sit and read or let my book slip out of my hands and daydream in peace. When I was as old as Granda I would be good like Granda. One day I would be like Aunty Jill, would be good and kind and everyone would come to me with their troubles and I would listen to them and help them. One day—but they were both old and I was still young. There were such heaps of things to do first. Later on I would listen to the serious things about Jesus and Good Friday and the things they tried to tell me about asking for help and trusting in Jesus.

Tonight I did not want to sit by Granda and listen to him playing. Tonight my own black cloud was coming between us.

"I think I'll go and take a bath, Granda," I said casually as soon as Aunty Jill and the Moorlands had gone.

Granda sat down and threw another log on the fire, sending sparks shooting up the back of the grate. He didn't answer at once and I didn't like just to walk away. Then he looked up at me.

"Can't you tell an old man what's troubling you, my Scrap? I liked that girl Sue, who was here this afternoon. She is a sensible sort of girl and a fine young Christian. She was telling me how she came to love Jesus. She'd be a grand friend to have, Janey. But I don't think you like her much, do you?"

For a moment I laid my head on his shoulder and felt his rough tweed jacket. For a moment I was a little girl again and could have told him anything. But I wasn't a little girl now, and I couldn't start to tell him. Bursting into tears I rushed out of the room and upstairs. Presently when I was lying soaking my pillow with crying I heard him start playing the piano and after a bit I lay quietly listening and thinking and planning. I *would* turn over a new leaf and be nice instead of nasty. Tomorrow I would find some way of clearing Sue's name, or at least of making amends to her somehow.

I sat up. My face was hot and puffy and my hair tousled. My new jumper was damp and rumpled with my tears and with wearing it on the bed. I undressed quickly and got into my dressing-gown. Perhaps my jumper would look all right if I hung it on the radiator while I took my bath. I always felt better when I was busy, and by the time I was splashing about in the bath I was much more cheerful. I even sang as I ran downstairs later to get the tea tray ready for our evening cup of tea, and was pleased to be ready to greet Aunty Jill almost as if nothing had ever been wrong.

CHAPTER SEVEN

THE RAIDERS

An answer to my new desire to put things right for Sue came much more quickly than I had expected. The real culprits of the thieving were planning something on a really big scale. They were going to raid the school canteen when the stores came in for the new month. I would never have known this, only I overheard Elaine Harper and Sylvia Rankin talking about it in the locker room. I had been kept behind after netball for some extra footwork because I was shaping well, and at first I thought the locker room was empty when I went in to change. Then I heard their voices and soon realised what they were saying.

Elaine and Sylvia were third-year girls and I did not like them. They refused to wear school uniform and the clothes they did wear seemed daft to Judy and Mary and me. We were proud of our uniform and enjoyed everything that made up school life for us. Elaine and Sylvia wore rings and ear-rings, and the staff got tired telling them to take them off because they only put them on again a few minutes later. We thought they were soft to behave like that.

From what I heard this raid was going to take place during a staff meeting, because the canteen would be left open for the staff to get a cup of tea afterwards. It would also be on the day of Sue's music lesson so that she would be the last person to be seen leaving the school. I kept absolutely still until Elaine and Sylvia went away and I was certain they had not seen me. I was thinking frantically how I could find out about the staff meeting and Sue's music lesson. Those were the two clues I simply had to solve.

I dashed up to my classroom and explained why I

was late. I had been kept for netball so that was all right. I took my place and tried to settle down to preparing English grammar for next day but my mind wasn't on it. I might be able to find out about Sue's music lesson, but I had no idea how to check up on a staff meeting.

We had all been working for about half an hour when the door opened and Monica London came in. She's a prefect and we all like her and think she is really great. She went up to Miss Hooper who shuffled her books and papers together and stood up. Then Miss Hooper called the preparation class to attention.

"Monica is taking my place until four o'clock as I have to attend a staff meeting. As you know, I expect you to behave with a prefect just as if I were here myself. Go on with your work."

I bent my head over my books but I couldn't work. The rest of the class had just blinked mildly at the announcement but it didn't mean anything much to them. A staff meeting? I was shaken. Could it possibly be today that the raid was going to take place? And how, oh how! could I do anything now to save Sue from getting caught?

I struggled with my English grammar and then tried my French, but I couldn't get on with either and I would have to take the work home or find some excuse for not having done it. At five minutes to four I heard a noise from the far end of the room. Sue was pushing books into her desk. I held my breath—I really did—I just couldn't believe it. She got up and walked up to Monica and I could hear every word she said. Sue never mumbled.

"Please, Monica, I have a music lesson at four, and Miss Hooper lets me go early to wash my hands. May I go now?"

Monica let her go and I was still taken aback when the bell rang and the scramble started for going home.

I shoved my books into my school bag and managed to shake off a very surprised Judy and Mary. We always waited for each other but I couldn't tell them about this and what I had to try to do. Pushing and barging my way against the stream of boys and girls making for the cloakrooms, I went to the canteen. I had to find Elaine and Sylvia and say something to stop them pinning anything on to Sue. I tore along the lower corridor which was empty because it led only to the kitchens and stores and canteen. I saw the two girls hanging around and they turned as I clattered up behind them.

"What do you want?" Elaine asked, obviously annoyed with me.

"You!" I panted. "I've got to tell you something. Sue's not like that."

"Who's not like what?" Elaine grabbed my arm and gave it a twist which hurt.

"Sue doesn't steal. You can't pin it on her, you can't!"

"Pin what on her? What are you talking about?"

She gave my arm another, sharper twist and I bit my lip. I wasn't going to cry out, whatever they did.

"The raid. I heard what you said and——"

"Clear out and keep your mouth shut!"

Sylvia came over. She was probably getting anxious about the time and wanted me out of the way.

"How do you know anything about Sue?" she asked.

"I just—I just—do."

"You'll have to tell us what you know."

Both girls were holding me now and my arms were very sore.

"I knew Sue years ago and she never did take things. When she came here I made out she did, but she never had. I know because it was me—I used to, but I never have here or at Maybank."

I was so desperate now I didn't care what I said so long as I could clear Sue.

Both girls roared with laughter.

"That's the best yet. O.K. Elaine, let her go, I believe her. She won't dare tell what she knows about us and the boys now we know that. You *are* green, kid. We've got something now that we can use whenever we want to, so just you keep your mouth shut or you will be in trouble. You are stupid! Now—run off—and remember!"

Sylvia let go of my arm and Elaine gave me a shove along the corridor. There was nothing for it but to go back to the deserted cloakroom and wait for Sue. When she did come I was in such a state that she could not make out what I was going on about. I didn't know that she had seen Elaine and Sylvia bullying me. She had come through the upper corridor while they were twisting my arm and she could see them from the windows there. She thought I was just upset and tried to calm me down.

"Come on, Janey; let's get out of here. It won't help if we get locked in, or a prefect finds us talking here."

Urging and pushing me along beside her, Sue managed to get us both out of school and round to the cycle shed. There seemed nothing more I could say. I was too muddled to be able to explain anything clearly. Our ways separated at the cross-roads and Sue gave me a cheery wave as she turned off to the left and called to me not to worry.

I cycled on slowly trying to decide what I ought to do and how I could possibly protect Sue from trouble. At least we had both been seen together, if anyone saw us leaving, but if the girls chose to say they had only seen Sue there wasn't much I could do.

I had got just beyond the park when Elaine and Sylvia rushed out at me from behind a tree. I tried to cycle on faster to get away from them, and then Pete —one of the boys I'd heard them name—came straight at me on his bike and rammed mine so that I toppled and fell against the kerb. I tried to pick myself up and he grabbed my machine and started twisting it all out of shape so that I would have to push it home. And all the time he kept talking at me, telling me what he would do to me and to Sue if I ever told anyone anything at all about today and what I had heard.

I was shaking all over now and terribly scared.

"What do you want?" I asked, reaching out to take my cycle away from him.

Pete laughed a nasty laugh.

"Just go home like a good little girl, Jane, and say you fell off your bike—you are quite crazy enough to do that!"

"I didn't!" I said hotly.

Pete shrugged his shoulders.

"Please yourself. I'm only doing you a kindness—warning you. Rod and Stan are round the next corner. If you don't do as I say they'll soon make you. Anyway, Elaine and Sylvie know enough about you now, so you'd better take my advice and be quiet."

Peter flung my bike at me and swung round and rode off, whistling to Rod and Stan to join him. They all looked back at me and had a good laugh as they saw me struggling with my damaged cycle and a bruise on my knee. My wrist was throbbing too and felt stiff and funny.

Elaine and Sylvia passed when the boys were out of sight, and Elaine started to tease me. Sylvia didn't say anything and after they had gone on and I had begun to try pushing my cycle Sylvia came back. She looked a bit upset and kept looking up the road to make sure no one saw her.

"Jane, I'm sorry, truly I am. I'd like to help you get home, but honestly I daren't. Here, I'll tie that wrist up with your scarf, how's that? I've only got five pence on me, but take it, Jane, and get a cuppa, The boys won't be at the café for ages yet."

I felt a bit better for Sylvia's kindness and I could see she meant it but I still didn't know what to do. I longed for Granda and Aunty Jill and yet I couldn't bear to have them see me in this state and I could never explain—not now and not ever, and they would be hurt and that would be worst of all. My wrist throbbed madly and so did my knee and my ankle. I couldn't walk fast and my cycle was so twisted that it wouldn't push straight and the pedals kept banging my shin. It was dusk now and I plodded on not thinking were I was going and not caring, when I found I was on quite the wrong road. I was utterly miserable and now I was so tired and sore that I started to cry and couldn't stop. It began to drizzle and I was cold and hungry.

A bright light shone behind me and I jumped. There hadn't been any cars on the road so far and I had forgotten about not having a light on my bike. We never left lamps on them in the cycle-shed and I was never out after dark as a rule and then only if Granda had seen that my lamps were on properly and working all right. The light came nearer and nearer and I tried to scramble on to the grassy bank at the side of the road. As I stumbled on the rough ground I lurched heavily on to my sore ankle and yelped with the pain as it gave way under me. I heard the squeal of car brakes, the clatter of my cycle against something hard, and I felt myself falling into darkness.

The next thing I knew was voices that seemed to be far away and then nearer and then away again. Men's voices that I couldn't recognise. One said something about 'a child missing after some trouble at the high school', and another said 'she was quite impossible to see—no lights at all—and just fell on to the road'. The voices went dim again and I missed the rest. I tried to move and yelped again. At once a man bent over me and I could see the shiny buttons of a policeman's uniform. Another man came over, too, but he was in ordinary clothes. He looked nice but worried. The policeman spoke to me.

"Come on, there's a lass. Can you tell me your name?"

"J—J—Janey T—Townsend," I managed to say between my chattering teeth.

"Fine. That's enough to go on with. Now, let's see what's wrong with you. Hurt anywhere?" He gently began to feel my bones and I yelped again when I tried to stand up.

"Leave her for now; we'll get an ambulance. My mate's got the radio going anyway; we'll soon get her tucked up in bed."

They covered me with a rug and I could hear the police radio crackling away in the police car that was behind the one that had come up behind me and frightened me. I had no idea how long all this had taken; I only knew it was now quite dark and the nice man seemed anxious to get on his way. I heard him say his wife would be worrying and I felt sorry for him. The policeman took a statement from him and then let him go. He came over and told me to cheer up and I'd be all right and then he drove off. By then the blue flashing light of an ambulance was coming towards us and I was feeling awful. The ambulance driver and the policeman lifted me into the ambulance and that was all I remembered of anything until I woke up in hospital and found Aunty Jill sitting by my bed and holding the hand that wasn't hurt.

When I opened my eyes I must have murmured something, because she bent over me quickly.

"Hush, darling! You are quite safe and it's all right. Go to sleep again and we'll talk when you feel better. I'm right here close beside you."

I did go to sleep again and I kept on sleeping most of the time for the next two days.

CHAPTER EIGHT

RECOVERY

It took me a long time to get well again. I had a broken wrist, a badly sprained ankle, several bruises and a severe chill that settled on my chest. Mummy came and stayed, and even Daddy came home in a hurry to see me. When I was well enough Mummy and Daddy had to go back but Aunty Jill and Granda spent hours visiting me. I got better slowly but there were lots of reasons why it was only slowly. Dr Moorland was the chest specialist and he went out of his way to be kind to me, and that worried me. Sue sent me messages and that worried me, too.

At first I had been asked to tell what had happened but I absolutely refused. When the doctors found that my temperature kept going up when I had been questioned they said I wasn't to be asked again until I was better. That was just as well, and yet it didn't solve anything. I wanted to know what had happened and how much anyone else knew. I wanted to tell Aunty Jill everything, but I didn't dare. I could guess that Pete had meant all the horrid things he had said and would easily carry out his threats.

At last I was allowed to go home and Sue was able to come in and out. I couldn't tell her my story and she wouldn't tell me hers. All she would say was that everything had died down at school and I'd better forget my troubles. Mr James had punished the boys for the raid and Sue herself was quite happy. She did say that she had told her parents the bit I had heard about the raid and they had taken her back to school and made her tell the Head. By then I was missing so some people had thought I was involved, but that was all she would say and after that she kept on changing the subject when I tried to find out anything else from her.

One afternoon after I was home again Aunty Jill was having a committee meeting of some sort in the house so she packed a picnic tea and suggested that Granda and I should go up on the downs and get some sunshine. We climbed slowly; Granda gave me plenty of time. He knew I liked to manage by myself even though I was still limping quite a bit, and he only put his hand out to help me over the really rough bits.

It was a marvellous day: the sky was clear, bright blue, larks were singing high up over our heads as they tumbled about in the sky. The woods smelled of warm pine resin, and under our feet was a soft carpet of pine needles. Behind us, when we turned round to look, lay the grey-blue water of the estuary, and sea-birds were whirling and swooping over the surface, calling out with their weird cries. Granda climbed over the stile first and set down the basket. Then he came back to help me over. I was managing fairly well but I was glad to feel his two strong hands steadying me as I clambered awkwardly over.

"Come, Scrap," he said, tucking my good arm into his. "Come and sit down and tell me all about it. You will have to soon, you know, and you'll never get really well until you do. You know your old Granda well enough to be able to tell me anything, now, don't you?"

I turned away from him and then as quickly turned back. He was right. I buried my head against his shoulder. I knew I had to tell.

"I must, Granda! I know I must, but I'm so frightened!"

Granda spread out the rug Aunty Jill had given us and helped me down on to it and then settled comfortably at my side. Slowly, and with lots of pauses and with Granda gently questioning me to keep me going, I told him everything—all about Sue and me and the raid and the boys and all that happened on that horrible journey home. Presently I stopped.

"Why did you want to get away from Aunty Jill and from me," he asked, sounding sad.

"From you most of all, Granda," I said.

"Why?"

"Because you've so often tried to help me and I've refused to listen. I wanted to be good like you and Aunty Jill, but not yet. That night I wanted to talk to Jesus and ask His help but I hadn't listened when you told me so I did not know how to find Him. Besides it's too late now. I'm too bad and when I'm old I'll probably be like Peter only worse, and not like Aunty Jill at all."

"You can never be too bad for Jesus, Scrap."

"But I am, Granda. Pete and the others are bad because I don't think they've anyone like you and Aunty Jill to help them—they don't seem to be that sort. But I have had help and I planned to be bad because I wanted to be—at least I didn't want to be good yet."

We sat without speaking for a bit and then Granda asked me if I had any more to tell.

"No, Granda, that's all."

"It's not really all. Listen while I tell you again. Remember we are all 'bad' in the first place and it was 'while we were sinners'—while we were still bad —'Christ died for us'. That is the truth and we must never, never doubt it. Jesus did not wait until we were nice enough or good enough. He knew He would have had to wait forever. God sent His Son Jesus to come and save us and lift us out of our sin into a new kind of life. He can make us really good with His own goodness. The night of your experience you were not found and brought home to safety after you had cleaned yourself up and made yourself tidy and well. You were found and brought back when you were lost and helpless, cut and bruised and dirty and sore.

There was nothing you could do to help yourself, was there?"

I shook my head. Granda was making it all so easy to understand.

"Well, that is how it always is, Janey. It has to be just as we are that we come to Jesus. We cannot hope to get clean and tidy first; we must ask Him to make us clean from inside."

"Really and truly, Granda?" I asked.

"Really and truly, Janey."

"Even for me, when I've been bad on purpose? Granda, wouldn't it be marvellous if we could start all over again. Ever since I took that money of Sue's I feel dreadful when I see a fifty-pence piece—I just can't ever forget."

"That's why we need Jesus. Knowing Him and loving Him and trusting Him does give us a clean start. You used to love playing with the old school slates in the attic, didn't you? You know how you can write and draw on them and then wipe them clean and begin all over again. When we tell Jesus we are sorry for what we have done wrong He wipes our lives clean and helps us to make a fresh start. Can you understand that?"

I sat very still, thinking it all over. Presently I put my hand into Granda's.

"Granda, will you stay here for a little and let me go on to our special rock round the corner, please? I'll be very careful but just now I'd like to go alone if you don't mind."

Granda got up and helped me to my feet and handed me his stout walking stick, and I knew he understood how I felt.

I struggled up over the rough ground and turned to wave just before I went round the corner and out of sight. Granda was sitting against a boulder and his head was bent so I could guess he was praying. I sat down carefully when I was sure I was quite alone.

This was a very beautiful spot and we had come up here together before this and once Granda had told me it was a place he came to when he wanted to be quite alone, and in a way I knew what he meant. It was very quiet.

This time I really had heard what Granda had been saying and every word had made sense. I couldn't go on the way I was—being miserable myself and making other people miserable—and now I knew I was making Jesus sad too for if He really loved me like Granda said I must have hurt Him when I wouldn't even listen to how He wanted to help me.

Now I was here I didn't know what to say. Of course I had said my prayers on and off since I was quite young and I had heard lots of people pray. I shut my eyes and thought about Granda and how easy it was to talk to him, so I started talking to Jesus in the same way and telling Him the things I'd told Granda. I asked Him to wipe my slate clean and let me begin all over again with His help. Presently I remembered Granda sitting alone and I got up to go back to him.

When I rounded the corner I saw that Sue had joined him. Granda said something to her and waved, and she sprang up and came leaping over the tufty grass to meet me.

"Hullo, Janey! I went round to your house and Miss Murray sent me up here."

"I'm glad, Sue! I'm glad about lots of things today. Granda's been talking to me and I'm sorry about everything that I've done wrong."

I think Sue guessed what I was meaning. She took my arm and guided me carefully and safely.

"I'm glad about lots of things, Janey, and I'm very glad we are friends."

"Oh, Sue, how nice of you to say that! I'm glad we are friends and there's so much for you to teach me. You know Jesus, and I'm only just beginning to find out."

Granda was unpacking the tea basket and looked up as we came nearer. We both shouted to him happily that we were hungry and he called back to us and waved. Then I saw him take out his handkerchief and wipe his eyes. He looked at me as we came up and it was a long and lovely look. I just said, in a whisper:

"Granda, the slate is wiped clean," and then I knew why he had been wiping his eyes. It was my first experience of knowing that one could cry because one was happy just as much as because one was sad.

We had a marvellous picnic and now that I had told all my story to Granda I found I wasn't scared any more, and because I had talked to Jesus I found I was really happy at last.